❖ TOYS COME HOME ❖

Toys Come Home

❧

Being the early experiences of

an intelligent stingray,

a brave buffalo,

and a brand-new someone called Plastic

❧

Emily Jenkins

illustrated by Paul O. Zelinsky

❧

schwartz & wade books · new york

Jen

Visit us on the Web! www.randomhouse.com/kids

Educators and librarians, for a variety of teaching tools, visit us at
www.randomhouse.com/teachers

Library of Congress Cataloging-in-Publication Data
Jenkins, Emily.
Toys come home / Emily Jenkins ; illustrated by Paul O. Zelinsky.—1st ed.
p.   cm.
Summary: When a little girl gets a plush stingray for her birthday, it makes friends with
some of her other toys as they all try to navigate in the world of real people.
ISBN 978-0-375-86200-7 (hardcover) — ISBN 978-0-375-96200-4 (glb) —
ISBN 978-0-375-89345-2 (ebook)
[1. Toys—Fiction. 2. Friendship—Fiction.] I. Zelinsky, Paul O., ill. II. Title.
PZ7.J4134 Toy 2011
[Fic]—dc22
2010005896

The text of this book is set in 13-point Archetype.

Printed in the United States of America

10 9 8 7 6 5 4 3 2 1

First Edition

For Ivy

—E.J.

For Rabbi' Keek

—P.Z.

Contents

✣

✢ TOYS COME HOME ✢

CHAPTER ONE

❧

In Which There Is Nowhere Nice to Sleep

StingRay has missed the birthday party.

She didn't mean to. It was her first party, first party ever in the world to be invited to—and she missed it.

She didn't even know she was missing it. She didn't know anything about the party until now, when it is already over.

She can tell the people are disappointed in her.

Here is what happened:

StingRay woke up. She had never been awake before, but she could hear a scissor scoring cardboard above her head. Opening a package mailed from a toy store. Inside the package, StingRay was squashed in a gift box that was wrapped in shiny blue paper and tied with a pink ribbon. She woke with a feeling that she'd been waiting, asleep, for a very long time.

She dreamed while she slept: the same dream over and over, about a wooden crate filled with other plush stingrays, packed with flippers touching flippers, tummies touching tails.

It was a mellow, cozy dream. The stingrays were still. The sounds were muffled.

A dream of something like a family, StingRay thinks.

Though she isn't entirely sure what a family is.

The word just came to her and she used it, inside her head.

I am an intelligent stingray, she thinks. To just have

a word come to me and to know it's the right word. In fact, now that I consider it, I know a lot of things! For instance,

I know that I'm a stingray,

and that a stingray is an extra-special kind of fish,

and that blue is the very best color anything can possibly be,

and that people are people,

and kids are baby people,

and that a kid would probably like to play with me someday.

I know all this stuff without being told. It's practically like magic, the knowledge I have.

I hope the rest of the world isn't too jealous of me.

The scissor scores the cardboard, and the wrapping is ripped off. Now StingRay comes out of her crispy nest of tissue paper and is pulled into the bright light of what she

knows, just knows somehow, is a kitchen. White cabinets. A jar of spoons and spatulas. Finger paintings stuck to the fridge with magnets.

A kid smiles down at her.

StingRay smiles back.

"She likes me!" says the Girl. "She smiled at me!"

"That's a nice pretend."

"I'm not pretending. She really did smile," the Girl insists.

The mommy kisses the Girl on her head. "Sorry it didn't come in time for your party. There was a shipping delay, Grandpa said when he called."

(A party? thinks StingRay. Was there a party?)

"Still, today is your actual birthday," the mommy goes on. "The day you were born. So it's nice to have a present on this day as well, isn't it?"

(I missed a party! thinks StingRay. A party I was supposed to go to!)

"Her name is StingRay," the Girl announces.

"Oh?" The mommy crinkles her nose. "Don't you want to call her a real name? Like Sophia or Samantha?"

"StingRay."

"Or maybe an animal name, like you gave Bobby Dot?"

(Who is Bobby Dot? wonders StingRay.)

"You could call her Sweetie Pie," continues the mommy. "Or Sugar Puff. How about Sugar Puff, hmm?"

"Just StingRay," says the Girl. "I like StingRay."

. . . . .

Upstairs, the Girl's bedroom has a high bed with fluffy pillows and a soft patchwork quilt. Atop the windowsill is a collection of birthday cards from her friends. There are shelves filled with books and games, puzzles and art supplies. A large ash-blue rocking horse resides in the corner. On the bed lie a plump stuffed walrus and a woolly sheep on wheels.

The sheep looks old.

Under the bookcase, StingRay can see several sets of tiny, sparkling eyes. She can feel them watching her. She can feel the eyes of the walrus, the sheep, and the rocking horse, too. But none of them is moving.

StingRay doesn't move, either.

The house feels big. Too big.

There don't seem to be any other stingrays here with whom to nestle. She longs for the comfort of her cozy dream.

The Girl sets StingRay on a low shelf and trots out of the room. She has a playdate.

When the family bangs the front door behind them and the toys can hear the rumble of the car starting in the driveway, the walrus galumphs himself to the edge of the bed, then hurls himself off. He executes a spectacular flip with a twist—and lands right side up.

Whomp!

He's a little larger than StingRay, and his plush is a

satiny walnut brown. His soft tusks and hairy gray whiskers are fresh and clean. The tag on his hind flipper reads DRY CLEAN ONLY.

The walrus shakes his head with a "Blubba-la blubba-la" sound, and the thick pudge of his neck rolls and shakes. Then he scoots over and snuffs his whiskery nose over the edge of the shelf where StingRay sits.

He doesn't speak.

StingRay doesn't speak.

StingRay has never spoken, though she would dearly like to. In fact, she thinks she might have a really huge amount to say. But she doesn't know how to get going, somehow.

"You say 'How dya do?' is what you say," the walrus announces eventually.

"Haaak," croaks out StingRay.

"No," snaps the walrus. "*'How dya do?'*" He repeats the phrase as if StingRay is stupid.

"How dya do?" StingRay manages.

"Splendiferous, thank you. And yourself?"

"Splendiferous." StingRay likes that word. It sounds grand.

"You can't say 'splendiferous' if I said 'splendiferous,'" complains the walrus. "You're doing it wrong."

"Sorry."

"I say 'splendiferous' and you say something *else*. Then you're not copying. Try again. How dya do?"

"Blue," says StingRay. "I'm blue, thank you."

"You're still doing it wrong," says the walrus. "It's not a question about color. But let's move on. My name is Bobby Dot. I was a birthday present and I arrived in the middle of an enormous party. The Girl really likes me and she sleeps with me on the high bed."

"My name is StingRay. I'm a birthday present, too."

"Stingray's not your name," says Bobby Dot. "Stingray's what you are."

"StingRay is too my name."

"Really?" Bobby Dot looks at her, pityingly.

"Yes." StingRay tries to hold her chin high, but she is wishing she were indeed called Sweetie Pie or Sugar Puff. Or even Sophia.

"Well. We can't all have real names, I suppose," says Bobby Dot as he hurls himself up onto the shelf with a thump. "Sheep is just called Sheep." He makes himself comfortable next to StingRay. "I don't think you *are* a birthday present, by the way."

StingRay is starting to find Bobby Dot unpleasant. "Why not?"

"Birthday presents come at birthday parties."

"The mommy said I was a birthday present."

"Well, maybe she said that to make you feel good. But if you were really a birthday present you would have arrived at the party."

StingRay knows he is right. She heard the people talking about how she'd failed to be at the party.

It is a bad feeling, this failure. Right at the start

of everything. So she pretends to know something she does not.

"I'm the Actual Day of Birth Present," she tells Bobby Dot. "Haven't you heard of that?"

The walrus draws his tiny bit of chin back toward his neck. "No."

"Oh." StingRay gives a shrill laugh. "I thought everybody knew about those! The Actual Day of Birth Present is this very special kind of blue present

      that arrives, of course, on the actual

      day of birth,

      not just on the day of the party, which is not

      very important,

      no offense.

      And the Actual Day of Birth Present is the

      present the kid wanted the most,

      in her very favorite color,

      in the best color in the world,

not walnut brown or anything boring

like that,

no offense.

I can't believe you didn't know about those.

I thought it was common knowledge."

StingRay has spoken so convincingly, she almost believes herself. Bobby Dot's bright new eyes dim slightly, and she feels a puff of satisfaction.

"Let's move on," the walrus says. "Here are some things about this house that you might want to learn."

StingRay sighs. She wishes she could tell Bobby Dot she already knows everything he could even think to tell her, but the truth is, she needs his information. She links her flipper with the one he's holding out and the two of them hop off the shelf. As they tour the room, the walrus points out important sights and landmarks. "Don't talk to the people," he says. "Just stay still and quiet when they're around. That's the bookshelf, make sure you put back anything you look at. The Girl pretty much knows about us. I mean, she talks to us. We just don't talk back. There's a TV downstairs. You can watch it when they're gone for the day but not at night because you might wake someone up. The bathroom is off the hall. There are some towels there and in the linen closet, but they keep to themselves, mostly. It's like a towel club or something. Not very nice. I wouldn't want to be a member."

StingRay follows Bobby Dot and remembers everything.

She still doesn't like him.

The tall rocking horse in the corner can't get around on his own, Bobby Dot explains, and he doesn't talk much. True to this description, the horse blinks his eyes and sniffs StingRay's proffered flipper to say hello, but he doesn't say "How dya do?" when she does.

A mischief of toy mice, very small in size, run across the floor to the toy box. The mice giggle among themselves and ignore StingRay. They proceed to pull out a box of small wooden blocks and play a lively game, squeaking and pushing the blocks about with their noses to make a maze. They move so fast StingRay cannot even count them.

"Mice!" cries Bobby Dot, clapping his front flippers together with authority.

The mice ignore him.

"I said, Mice!" He claps again.

Still no response.

Bobby Dot heaves his thick body up and down repeatedly, making heavy banging noises on the carpet.

Whomp!

Whomp!

Whomp!

"Mice, pay attention. I am talking to you!"

The mice pause briefly, a couple of them balancing on top of blocks. A plump white one chews on his own tail.

"This is StingRay," announces the walrus. "She is a

marine animal like me. She has come here to stay. Please give her your attention and courtesy."

"Sheesh," mutters the plump white mouse. "You'd think he'd lived here forever, the way he acts."

Whomp! "Tell her 'How dya do!'" shouts Bobby Dot, thumping his body again.

The mice, unafraid but wanting to go back to their game, squeak "How dya do" at StingRay.

"Let's move on," says Bobby Dot.

. . . . .

The Girl and her family return in the evening, and when night falls the dad reads a book about a cat and a doll who live in a tree with a large collection of hats. StingRay listens to the story from her spot on the low shelf. Bobby Dot and Sheep are up on the bed where they can see the pictures.

Then the dad turns out the light and sings until the Girl's eyes fall shut.

The first day is over.

Sheep and Bobby Dot are asleep on the high bed, now. StingRay wants to sleep, too. In fact, she is very sleepy, but she can't relax, can't get comfortable on her hard, lonely shelf.

The toy mice emerge and scuttle about. They pull down a book and open it in front of the horse, who rocks gently as he reads in the near-darkness. The mice begin leapfrogging over one another, squeaking softly. Every now and then the plump white mouse scoots over and flips a page in the horse's book.

StingRay thinks about going down the hall to meet the towels, but she is nervous that they won't be friendly, after what Bobby Dot said.

She also isn't sure what a towel is.

What if it has sharp teeth?

What if it has angry claws?

What if the vicious towels become enraged when a plush stingray tries to join their private conversation?

They might rip her to shreds and eat her for dinner. Or jump on her with their huge, hairy feet

until she's completely flat,

then hang her on their wall for decoration.

She stays where she is.

After a while, the rocking horse shuts its long-lashed eyes and the toy mice scuttle under the bookshelf to go to bed. StingRay flops down and peers under the shelf at their shining eyes. Maybe she could get to sleep if she slept with them! All one on top of the other like in the dream about the box of other stingrays.

"Hi," she whispers.

"Oh. Hello there, marine animal!" shouts one mouse. "We're going to bed now. Night-night!"

"I was wondering. Could I sleep with you?" says StingRay. It is hard for her to ask. She chokes out the words.

"Sure!" cries the mouse. "Come on in!"

So StingRay, feeling awkward and grateful, tries to shove her big plushy body into the narrow flat space beneath the bookshelf.

One flipper goes in. And the tip of her nose.

"We'll push you!" cries a mouse.

They swarm out from underneath the shelf and begin pushing StingRay with their hard little mouse noses.

They grunt with the effort.

The rest of StingRay's nose goes in, plus some more flipper. "There!" cries one mouse.

"Great pushing, guys!" cries another.

"We pushed the marine animal. Did you see? Did you see? We pushed it!"

"I saw. I was pushing with you."

"We pushed it with our noses! High five!"

StingRay's face is jammed against the shelf, but out of the corner of one eye, she can see the mice bouncing up and down, pleased with themselves.

"I'm not in," she says.

"You're *almost* in!" cries a brown mouse. "You just have to make yourself a bit smaller."

Maybe this is the sort of thing a stingray can do if she tries, StingRay thinks. So she smallens herself, lessens herself, scrunches herself down and diminishes with all her might.

"A little more smaller!" yells the mouse. "Then you'll be in!"

StingRay tries again, but somehow, she does not diminish. She stays exactly the same.

Maybe it is not the sort of thing a stingray can do if she tries.

"I think I'll just sleep here," says StingRay. "Because, you know, stingrays like to sleep out in the cold dark air. We like that better than cozy under bookshelves."

"Nighty-night, then!" cries a mouse, and they all scuttle under the shelf and make themselves comfortable.

StingRay can feel their hard, furry bodies bumping her nose and creeping back and forth across her one flipper that is underneath. It is ticklish. And not at all cozy.

Eventually, the mice settle down and go to sleep, but StingRay can't see or feel any of them. She waggles her flipper around a bit, looking for a cuddly mouse to comfort her as she tries to rest.

"Marine animal!" She hears a squeak. "Marine animal!"

"What?"

"You are hurting me with your big arm!"

"And you are squashing *me* with your nose on my bed!" cries another voice.

StingRay's face feels hot and she pulls both her nose and flipper out from under the bookshelf.

"Thank you!" "Nighty-night!" cry the mice.

"Good night," says StingRay.

She goes back to her shelf and settles herself there for the night. All alone, she sleeps only fitfully.

· · · · ·

When the Girl goes to school the next day, she takes Bobby Dot with her and leaves Sheep down on the floor.

Sheep is gray-white and ancient, with four wooden wheels, two felt ears, and a firm wool body. "Before I came here I was Dad's favorite toy—and Grandpa's before that," she says, by way of introduction. "What were you?"

StingRay wasn't anything before this. This is all she ever was.

"I was . . . I was . . . ," she stutters.

Sheep sniffs. "You have a new-toy smell, same as that walrus," says Sheep. "Is that it? You're a new toy?"

StingRay does *not* want to have the same smell as Bobby Dot.

"I was the mommy's," she lies. "And that is not new-toy smell you're smelling. That is extremely clean smell,
    plus roses and geraniums and clover
    and everything fresh and lovely and precious.
    It is a special smell for toys that are loved a
    huge entirely lot.

Bobby Dot smells like plastic thread and
sawdust,

I know what you're talking about,

but that is not my smell at all."

Sheep sniffs again. "I like clover," she says, agreeably.
"And geraniums. I would like to chew some one day, but
I don't suppose it'll ever happen."

Since Sheep seems friendly, StingRay asks her to play
a game—and Sheep agrees. But before StingRay can read
the instructions and get the checkers set up (Sheep hasn't
got flippers or arms that she can use), there is a gentle
snore from the other side of the board.

Sheep is asleep.

StingRay pokes her new friend with a flipper.

She barks "Hello!" in Sheep's felt ear and even pulls
her scrawny tail.

But waking Sheep is impossible.

Slowly, StingRay puts the checkers back in the box.

. . . . .

That night, exhausted, StingRay tries to sleep next to the rocking horse. She creeps across the rug to him and announces, "I'm just going to keep you company here.

Because you seem like you might be lonely.

Like, you want to have someone to sleep next to you, so the night doesn't seem so long.

I am going to help you out with that."

She drapes one soft flipper over the lower rail of the horse's base.

But it is not very cuddly.

So she climbs, pushing with her tail and clinging with her flippers, onto the horse's back, then relaxes into the saddle.

But it is kind of wobbly.

She flops onto the horse's head and flips around to face the other way, so that her long tail trails across his nose and her warm flippers embrace his ears.

The horse coughs.

"What?" StingRay whispers.

"No thank you."

"Oh, come on. It'll be so nice! You won't feel lonely anymore!"

"No *thank you*," says the horse firmly. Then he shakes his head, the way horses do to ward off flies. His mane swings out and his nose arcs through the air and StingRay is flung sharply across the room to land—

on the high bed with the fluffy pillows.

Hooray! This is perfect.

StingRay can sleep with Sheep, Bobby Dot, and the Girl!

Carefully, carefully she creeps up to the head of the bed. Sheep is clutched in the Girl's chubby palm, Bobby Dot is under the covers.

Both of them wake as StingRay settles herself between them.

"I was dreaming of clover," mutters Sheep, sleepily.

"I was dreaming of sharks," whispers Bobby Dot, irritably.

"I'm going to sleep on the high bed now!" announces StingRay, trying to sound confident. "Because I'm the Actual Day of Birth Present. We're all going to be cuddling together from now on!"

Sheep eyes Bobby Dot. "It's already a lot more crowded here than it used to be," she says, meaningfully. "Before the birthday, there was plenty of room in this bed."

Bobby Dot eyes Sheep right back. "It would be fine if some people didn't have hard wooden parts," he says.

"It would be fine," says Sheep, "if some people didn't have teeth that are way larger than regular teeth that people have. And also if those people with the teeth didn't talk so much all the time when other people are trying to rest."

"I don't have teeth," says StingRay. "Or wooden parts.

I'm an extremely cuddly stingray. And you won't believe how quiet I can be."

She looks hopefully at Sheep.

Sheep has already gone back to sleep.

"*I'm* going to be awake for hours," complains Bobby Dot. "I can't believe you woke us like this. Don't you know it's sleepytime?"

Fine then, thinks StingRay.

Meanie.

Suddenly, she doesn't want to cozy up with Bobby Dot and Sheep anymore. She doesn't want to sleep anywhere in this cold unfriendly room. Or anywhere in this too-big house.

That's it. StingRay is running away.

Right now. Running away forever and ever.

Without another word to Bobby Dot, she flops off the bed and lurches toward the door.

She'll go away from these selfish toys to somewhere better. Much better.

And she'll never come back!

And then they'll all miss her!

Without thinking about the herd of possible vicious towels in the linen closet and the bathroom, without thinking about where she will go and how she will sleep, StingRay zooms out of the Girl's bedroom, down the hall and—

Fwap! Gobble-a gobble-a.

Fwap! Gobble-a gobble-a.

Fwap! Gobble-a gobble-a.

Bonk!

Falls down the stairs. Flipper over flipper, thumping and ouching, bouncing off moldings and posts, then lying shocked at the bottom, head aching.

But she cannot rest. She is running away. Where to go? Where to go?

StingRay has not been in the downstairs of the house since she arrived. She doesn't remember which room is the kitchen, the living room, anything. She hurls herself across the wood floor, searching for an exit in the dark.

She can feel something swing slightly as she bangs into it, so she pulls up short. It's a door. The door to the outside.

This is it.

Eyes shut tightly, StingRay pushes through the doorway and down another flight of stairs—

Fwap! Gobble-a gobble-a.

Bonk!

—to land in complete darkness.

The floor underneath her is cold.

StingRay coughs.

It is very dusty.

There is a rumbling coming from the other end of the room.

This is not the outside. StingRay has looked out the

windows enough to know that the outside has grass and trees and the sounds of cars going by, leaves rustling. Here, she can hear nothing but the scary rumble.

This must be the basement.

Rumble. Ruuuuuuumble.

What is that sound?

Could it be a ghost?

Maybe ghosts go to the basement to hide when the attic gets full up, StingRay thinks.

Maybe they go down there to eat marine animals

who might have strayed from their usual habitats,

or make slaves of lonely friendless people.

Maybe it's not ghosts at all but axe murderers, leaping around with axes and rumbling all about how they want to chop things.

Whooooo addleaddleaddle!

Something hairy with lots of legs crawls onto Sting-Ray's flipper. She can feel it inching its way across. . . .

It is on her! The thing! Maybe a spider with fifty-eight legs,

just a crazy amount of creepy crawly legs,

and it is crawling on StingRay's body—

Whooooo addleaddleaddle! StingRay rears up and flaps her flippers and screeches to get the spider off. Oh, it sends shivers down her back! She rolls in the dust and flops back and forth and tosses her head—eeeeewwwww— and finally, finally comes to a stop when she is sure the spider-thing is not on her anymore.

In the darkness, she can just make out stacks of cardboard boxes looming on either side of her.

She has lost her bearings.

Where are the stairs?

She is scared to move.

She can still hear that rumble ruuuuuuumble, and if she moves, the ghosts and/or axe murderers might notice her.

She curls herself up as tight as she can, tucking her tail around her body, and holds perfectly still.

After a minute or two, there is a loud buzz. The rumble stops.

StingRay waits for it to start again, but it does not. Still, she is scared to look for the stairs. Instead she sits, tense and knotted, for hours, until the morning sun shines softly through the high basement windows and she hears footsteps on the floor above her.

Feet come softly down to the basement and pad over to the dryer. The dad fills a basket with clothes and turns to take it upstairs. "Honey, your stingray is down here!" he calls in surprise.

He picks StingRay up and brushes some dust from her plush, then places her on top of the basket. Bouncing up the steps, two at a time, he delivers StingRay into the waiting arms of the Little Girl.

"Oh, sweetie sweetie!" cries the Girl, hugging StingRay. "I thought you were lost! I looked for you all over this morning." She plants a kiss on StingRay's head. "Now, remember this from now on: don't go in the basement or I will miss you, miss you! I need you very much."

The Girl smells like maple syrup and soap. Her arms are warm on StingRay's cold, tight body.

This is what StingRay has been looking for.

Somebody to love.

Somebody who will love her back.

Who will be her family.

Of course, the Girl is it. Of course she is.

StingRay should have known that all along.

She relaxes into the Girl's embrace and feels the beautiful day stretch before her as she is carried into the kitchen to watch waffles being made.

CHAPTER TWO

※

The Story of an Ear

As winter fades and spring blooms, StingRay spends most of her time indoors—learning to play checkers against herself, watching TV, playing with the Girl, listening to stories, nodding while Bobby Dot lectures.

Now the rains have stopped and the air is hot with the smell of earth and grass. It is finally summer. Today StingRay, Sheep, and Bobby Dot are in the backyard.

There is a cluster of flowering rosebushes by the fence. The songs of birds and the buzz of mosquitoes.

The Girl and her mother go in and out of the house, bringing lemonade, a picnic blanket, and a parasol. The sun is warm and sinking in the sky.

A big kid comes over to play with the Girl. She is called Bethany and her hands seem very large to StingRay. She can stand on her hands, this big kid. And do a cartwheel.

Her voice is too loud.

The Girl and Bethany dig some holes and make roads for a couple of toy cars. They turn somersaults while the mommy reads a book.

"Let's play ball!" says Bethany, her hair full of grass. (Sheep is eyeing the grass and making tiny, almost invisible chewing motions with her jaw.)

"I don't have a ball," says the Girl.

"Everybody has a ball," says Bethany.

"I don't."

(What's a ball? StingRay wonders.)

"We had a ball," says the mommy. "But we lost it at the park. Why don't you toss one of your animals?"

Bethany grabs Sheep and throws her up in the air, catching her neatly in both hands.

(A ball must be a kind of animal, thinks StingRay.)

"Maybe not Sheep," says the mom. "She's old. And you could hurt yourself on her wheels."

"She's a flying sheep!" cries Bethany, tossing Sheep to the Girl.

(A ball is a flying animal. StingRay thinks she knows all about it now.)

The mommy goes inside, muttering something about maybe having a tennis ball somewhere that would make a better choice.

Bethany throws Sheep. Blop!

The Girl throws Sheep back. Blop!

And again. And again.

Sheep is frightened. StingRay can see it. Her hard

black eyes bulge in terror and her neck is tucked as tight into her woolly body as she can get it.

Blop.

Aaaaaaand blop.

Aaaaaaand blop. Sometimes they drop her, or miss the catch entirely. Then Bethany and the Girl run laughing across the lawn, grab Sheep from the ground, and—

Blop! Blop!

Keep playing.

"They shouldn't do that!" StingRay whispers to Bobby Dot.

Bobby Dot grunts.

"Really!" StingRay is outraged. "It's like they don't even know she has feelings!"

"Better her than me," the walrus whispers.

"Not better her than you. She's old! She could break."

"On the contrary," says Bobby Dot. "She's survived for years. Sheep is built to last."

"Shouldn't we stop it?" says StingRay.

"What can we do?" says Bobby Dot. "Anyway, she probably likes it."

But StingRay can tell that Sheep does not.

Blop.

Aaaaaaand blop.

Aaaaaaand bang! Sheep is thrown too far and too hard! She hits the wooden fence and falls down—scrabble, scrabble, scriiiiitch—through the fat yellow blossoms and into the arms of the rosebush.

All is silent. The children walk over and have a look.

"It's thorny," Bethany announces. "Your mom is going to have to get her out."

The Girl looks at Sheep, hanging in a tangle of branches. "Is she okay?"

"She's fine," says Bethany.

"I think she's hurt," says the Girl. "I'm sorry, Sheep."

"She's fine."

"Kids! Dinner's ready," calls the Girl's father, opening the screen door. He trots down the back steps and collects the empty lemonade bottles, the parasol, and the picnic blanket. "Go on in. Spaghetti and tomato sauce."

"Pasghetti!" yells the Girl. She scoops up Bobby Dot and runs into the house with Bethany close behind her.

The sun is setting. StingRay and Sheep are alone in the yard. StingRay can hear the sounds of the family, plus Bethany and Bethany's dad, eating spaghetti and talking. Glasses clink. A piece of silverware clatters to the floor. People laugh.

"Someone will come outside and get us, right?" StingRay asks Sheep.

Sheep bleats, softly. Pitifully.

"Yes, someone will." StingRay answers her own question. "Just like someone came and got me from the basement. Don't worry. The Girl won't be able to sleep without you, Sheep. She needs you in the high bed with her," says StingRay, though that last sentence catches in her throat.

Sheep only bleats.

The two of them listen as the humans eat peach cobbler and the kids dance around the living room to a song about "glorious mud."

They listen as Bethany and her father say good night and drive away in their car.

They listen as the people head upstairs and the Girl runs water in the bathroom. They can hear her splash in the tub. They can even hear the whizz of her electric toothbrush. Then the dad reading aloud.

And the dad singing.

The parents chatting downstairs. Washing dishes.

Going to bed.

"Okay. No one is coming," says StingRay finally. "But they'll come in the morning. I mean, they know where we are. And we're not even anywhere scary. So that's good."

Sheep just bleats. And the bleat sounds frantic.

Sheep actually *is* somewhere scary, remembers Sting-Ray. She is in a thorny bush.

StingRay flops over, the cool night grass tickling her

tummy. Looking up, she sees that a single huge thorn pierces one of Sheep's felt ears. Sheep is suspended by her ear from that thorn, her body and her wheeled platform dangling down through the branches.

"Does it hurt?" asks StingRay.

Sheep bleats.

Okay.

This is serious.

StingRay must rescue Sheep. Sheep—who is not really even StingRay's friend; Sheep, who does not want StingRay to sleep on the high bed; Sheep, who keeps falling asleep while StingRay is *talking*; Sheep, who isn't the sort of person to care a whole lot about anybody else's loneliness but spends her days gently nibbling one corner of the Girl's box spring or sometimes a shoelace—Sheep is in trouble. And it doesn't matter, suddenly, that Sheep has never helped StingRay.

StingRay will help Sheep.

But if StingRay climbs the thorn bush, her good-looking plush will get thorns in it.

Plus, she might get stuck.

Even if she did get up to the branch, it is not clear that StingRay's flippers will be able to unhook Sheep's ear from the thorn.

"Slingshot."

What? Did Sheep bleat something? StingRay was thinking important thoughts.

"Slingshot."

StingRay knows what a slingshot is. She and Sheep and Bobby Dot saw one on television the other day, while the Girl was at school and the grown-ups at work. It is a contraption where you get yourself a big rubber band and a rock;

you stretch the rubber band around the rock,

and you attach ends of the stretched rubber

band to two sticks in the ground,

and then you streeeeeeeeetch the rubber band

and the rock back together soooooo far—

and let go.

Then the rock zings through the air and hits your enemies on the head!

Hopefully.

"What are you yammering about?" StingRay asks Sheep. "There is no slingshot here. There's not even a rubber band."

"Leg warmer."

"I am trying to figure out how to help you," says StingRay, irritably. Sheep must be talking nonsense from the stress of being hung in a thorny bush.

"Leg warmer."

Oh.

StingRay sees it now, in the dark. A sparkly blue leg warmer is indeed lying on the grass, halfway under a bush.

"Very pretty, but I'm problem-solving here."

"Slingshot." Sheep's bleat is feeble but persistent.

StingRay investigates the leg warmer. It is stretchy and quite long.

Like a rubber band.

Sheep wants her to build a slingshot. (Who would ever imagine that Sheep had the brains to think of it?)

"I'm going to rescue you with a leg warmer!" cries StingRay.

She gets to work. First she ties one end of the leg warmer to one post of the back-porch stair rail. Then she takes the other end of the leg warmer in her mouth and ties it around the other post, pulling it tight.

Then she wiggles herself into the center of the stretched warmer, and scootches up the steps until it is pulled as far back as it can possibly go. She is only holding herself in place by pushing down hard, hard with her tail.

Frrrrrr, Frrrrrr, Frrrrrr.

StingRay hears herself making this sound in the back of her throat.

It is a fear noise. Because she could slingshot herself toward where Sheep is hanging from the rosebush and—

Miss.

She could hit the bush full-on and end up covered in thorns.

She would be a thorny stingray forever and ever after that,

> and everyone would call her Pokey because
> she was always poking them with her thorns.
> Or she could hit the fence behind the bush,
> and be flattened into the shape of a waffle.
> People would put butter and syrup on her
> and cut her into bite-sized pieces,
> or worst of all,
> she could go over the fence and be lost
> forever in the yard of strangers.

StingRay is about to ease herself out of the slingshot

and just slither up the steps to wait sweetly on the doorstep for the people to find her in the morning, when Sheep bleats again. It is such a soft, sad bleat, it doesn't even have a proper "b" in it.

"*Aaaaa,*" Sheep cries. "*Aaaaa.*"

StingRay stops thinking. She releases the leg warmer and launches herself across the yard,

Whoooooosh! Through the air,

bouncing off the garage,

twisting and turning—

zooping down to where Sheep hangs from the thorny branch.

Whap! StingRay grabs Sheep in her plush flippers and holds on as hard as she can to the woolly body as they hurtle, with a slight ripping sound, down to the ground, landing in the dirt beneath the rosebush.

They lie there together, Sheep and StingRay. Looking up through the dark.

StingRay glows with pride.

Rescue completed.

Rescue with a leg warmer!

Rescue from the horrible thorny bush.

Oh.

Wait.

Gazing up, StingRay sees Sheep's softy ear.

It is still attached to the thorn.

"Look," she says in quiet shock. "Look, Sheep. Your ear."

Will Sheep yell at her? Maybe Sheep will call StingRay names and scold her for careless ear-losing. Weep and scream over that lovely ear that is so badly torn it can never be sewn on again.

StingRay waits, tense, for Sheep to begin yelling.

But Sheep says nothing.

Finally, StingRay flops over and peers, close up, at Sheep's face. A small snore floats from Sheep's nostrils. She is asleep.

. . . . .

In the early dawn, before any people in the house have woken up, Sheep opens her eyes.

Grass. There is unlimited grass here. And nobody to see her chewing it.

Nom nom nom.

Nom nom nom nom, nom nom nom!

Ooh, and clover.

Nom nom nom.

Sheep chews her way over to StingRay and gives her a gentle nudge. "Wake up. No one can see you. You can chew the grass!"

Oof. StingRay is sleepy and sore from the slingshot.

Grass doesn't interest her.

"Or do you like clover? You can chew the clover!"

StingRay doesn't even have teeth, but she raises her eyes politely. "How does your head feel?" she asks.

"What?" bleats Sheep. "I can't hear you. I've lost my ear."

"HOW DOES YOUR HEAD FEEL?"

Nom nom nom nom, nom nom nom. "Actual grass. Can you believe it?"

"I AM SORRY ABOUT YOUR EAR!" cries StingRay.

"You don't have to shout. The other ear still works," says Sheep. Then, unexpectedly, she leans her head sweetly against StingRay's flank. "Oh. I never thought I'd get grass," she says, sighing. "I never thought it."

"That's nice."

"This is the best day of my life," says Sheep.

"It is?" StingRay knows Sheep has been around a long time.

"Yes, it is. You, me, and a yard full of grass," says Sheep.

CHAPTER THREE

✣

What Happened to Bobby Dot

It is now three months later. Sheep has forgotten how it felt to ever have a matching set of ears, but she remembers the grass very well and talks about it often. The clover, too.

StingRay plays solitaire with a deck of cards she's secreted under the bed. She also spends hours looking out the Girl's window at the neighborhood below, wishing for someone interesting to talk to.

The leaves have begun to turn red, orange, and brown. Pumpkins are perched fatly on people's front steps. People huddle in jackets and scarves. It is fall.

Today, the Girl is sick. It started with feeling hot in the face on Thursday, then a fever and Friday staying home. Then a sore stomach and now the Girl is puking.

Her dad comes running as she starts, but it is too late. She has thrown up all over Bobby Dot, who was cuddling with her on the high bed. The vomit covers his thick whiskers, his long tusks, his insufferably self-satisfied eyes. It covers his chubby plush body, sparing only his back flippers.

"Here, take your towel," says the dad, rubbing the Girl's back. He hands her a large rectangle of yellow terry cloth, which she uses to wipe her mouth and hands.

The dad tosses Bobby Dot and the soiled patchwork quilt onto the floor near where StingRay is watching. He and the Girl head down the hall to the bathroom.

"Excuse me," whispers StingRay to the walrus. "Was that a *towel*?"

"Puke! Puke! I'm covered in puke!" Bobby Dot does not answer the question.

"Because *you* said towels had teeth and claws—"

"I can't believe she puked on me. Ug! So disgusting!"

"—and that was just a big terry-cloth rectangle. You told me they were vicious!"

"Oh, it smells. Can you smell me? Do I smell like puke?"

"You're telling me the whole scary towel gang is nothing but a club of rectangles?"

"Yes, it's a club of rectangles!" Bobby Dot barks. "Very obnoxious rectangles who do their rectangle thing and sing together and aren't very welcoming! How could you not know what a towel is?"

"I knew," lies StingRay. "I knew what a towel was. I just thought these ones at this house had teeth and claws, because *that is what you told me!* The only reason I was confused is because you lied."

"I am covered in puke! I can't worry about your problems. Can you believe the Girl puked on me?"

"She's *sick*," snaps StingRay. "She couldn't help it."

"She could have turned away. She could have just puked on the blanket. She was thoughtless."

"She puked on you with love!" StingRay is outraged. "She was cuddling you on the high bed to make herself feel better!"

"This is the most disgusting experience of my life," moans Bobby Dot.

"It is an honor to be puked on by the Girl." StingRay rears up in anger. "You are not appreciating what an honor it is. I would give anything to be up on that high bed, being puked on and cuddled."

At that moment, the dad and the Girl return from the bathroom.

Dad tosses the vomity yellow towel onto the pile of Bobby Dot and the patchwork quilt. He helps the Girl put on a clean nightgown and get back under the sheets. Then he scoops up the linens and the walrus, and heads downstairs to do laundry.

. . . . .

Bobby Dot does not return that day.

Neither does the towel.

Neither does the patchwork quilt nor the dirty nightgown.

The Girl sleeps under a crocheted afghan with the one-eared sheep.

She does not puke any more.

The next morning, the dad brings back the linens from the washer and dryer in the basement. He puts the patchwork quilt on the bed and hangs the worn yellow towel in the hall bathroom. The Girl is feeling well enough to go play downstairs, so the toys are left alone.

"Where is Bobby Dot?" asks StingRay.

Nobody answers.

"Sheep, did you hear me?"

Apparently, Sheep did not.

"Mice, where is Bobby Dot?" calls StingRay. "Rocking Horse? Does anybody know?"

"He went to the basement to get washed," squeaks a tiny voice from under the bookcase.

"Yes. Well. We know that. We all know that," says StingRay. "The question is, where is he *now*? Because he hasn't come back and the basement is full of spiders and maybe ghosts."

Nobody answers.

"If you don't have any suggestions for me," announces StingRay, "then I'll have to go down the hall and ask that yellow towel."

Again, no answer.

Oh.

Now StingRay has to go ask the towel.

It is not nearly so scary a prospect as when she thought

towels had teeth and claws, but she remembers what Bobby Dot said about them being clubby and unfriendly, and she wishes she had not just announced that she would talk to one.

Still, Bobby Dot has not returned.

And StingRay needs to know what happened.

She waits until night. Until the Girl is asleep and the house is quiet. Then she scoots down the hall and peers nervously into the bathroom. StingRay has never been in there before, and she is surprised at how very tile-y it is. Tile on the floors. Tile on the walls. There is a smell of tangerine soap. The black-and-white whales printed on the shower curtain look menacing.

The yellow towel, damp and slightly wrinkled, hangs over the shower rod. Some floating bath toys are lined up on the edge of the tub: a boat, an orca, two pirates, a purple spray bottle, and a squirty rocket.

StingRay addresses the pirates. "Ahoy. My name is

StingRay. I am looking to talk to the yellow towel in hopes of investigating the disappearance of a walrus."

No reply.

"What I need to know is: Is this towel friendly? Do you think I can just ask it a question?"

Again, no reply.

"Or do I need an introduction?" StingRay goes on. "Or, like, membership in a club?"

"It's friendly," says a voice from above. A soothing, droopy voice.

StingRay looks up.

The towel is speaking to her. "None of those bath toys talk," she continues. "But I do. My name is Tuk-Tuk."

"Hello," says StingRay. "I—I'm wondering about the walrus. Bobby Dot. Do you remember? He was covered with puke and he went down to the basement for a wash, but—"

"He never came back." TukTuk finishes the sentence. StingRay nods.

"They should never have put him in the Dryer."

"What's a dryer?"

"Dries towels and clothes after we're done in the washing machine. Everything spins around very hot."

"Why shouldn't Bobby Dot have gone in?"

"The Dryer is very sensitive. They should never have put in those sneakers, either."

"What happened?"

"I was in the load ahead of him. He washed up okay, even though his tag said Dry Clean Only. I saw him come out of the washer clean and fresh."

"And then?"

"The Dryer can't handle sneakers."

"TELL ME WHAT HAPPENED!" StingRay shouts, and is surprised to see the towel's edges curl up slightly in recoil.

For a moment, TukTuk doesn't answer. Then she

says: "The Dryer's barrel got out of line. Started thumping. No one came. She went through the whole cycle. When the dad unloaded, the walrus was in shreds."

StingRay is so shocked she can't speak.

"He was nothing but fluff and scraps of plush," says TukTuk. "The rest was clogging up the lint collector." She sighs. "Maybe the threads that held him together were plastic. Maybe those threads melted. Or could be all that shaking was just too much."

"Oh."

"They threw what was left of him in the trash," TukTuk finishes. "But he was gone long before that happened."

Oh, oh, oh.

Bobby Dot is gone.

Bobby Dot will never, ever come back.

StingRay tries to feel sad, because she is pretty sure that's how you are supposed to feel, but fear washes over her instead. Fear, like a cold wave that creeps up her tail and across her belly. Frrrrrr, Frrrrrr.

Because now StingRay knows something she really and truly did not know before. A life can be over.

"Was he your friend?" asks TukTuk gently. "I'm very sorry."

"No," says StingRay, truthfully. "But he was the Girl's friend."

. . . . .

The other toys take the shredding of Bobby Dot very calmly. "Too bad, too bad. But no one lasts forever," squeaks one toy mouse, and the others take up her cry: "No one lasts forever! No one lasts forever!" until one of them spots a Cheerio dropped on the rug and scoots over to practice chewing it. The others follow to lend encouragement.

The rocking horse just nods seriously when StingRay tells him. And Sheep opens one eye from her slumber to ask, "Bobby who?"

"The walrus."

"The walrus who used to be here a long time ago?"

"He was here yesterday morning."

Sheep squints. "I thought it was a long time ago. What did you say happened with him?"

StingRay can't face explaining it again. She changes the subject.

The toys don't care much, but the Girl is bereft. When her parents tell her what happened to Bobby Dot, her face swells with all the crying. She whimpers "Walrus, walrus" before bed each night, and starts the morning with a solemn look on her face. Even after her health improves, she looks wan.

On the third day of this grief, the Girl picks up StingRay at bedtime and takes her to the high bed. She sobs a bit—"Walrus, walrus"—but snuggles her damp face against StingRay's soft plush body and seems consoled.

The high bed! Specialness!

The Girl! Wants StingRay!

On the high bed!

Oh, specialness, specialness!

Being up there, cuddling and falling asleep, is the best feeling StingRay has ever had in her short life.

And yet, she wakes up in the middle of the night. Thinking about Bobby Dot. Thinking about how, now that he's gone, she feels as if she's supposed to have liked him. As if she should remember nice things about the departed.

Only, she didn't like him.

Sometimes, she even wished he would disappear so she could sleep on the high bed instead of him.

And now he has.

Now StingRay—who thought Bobby Dot so horrid for saying "Better her than me" when Sheep was being thrown across the yard—now StingRay herself is thinking: "Better him than me." Thinking it quite a lot, actually.

It is a bad thought.

But sleeping on the high bed is good.

Now, while the Girl is sad, StingRay is happy.

Does that make StingRay a bad person?

The joy, the guilt, the loss, and the relief: all these feelings toss around inside her in the night, while StingRay stares at the ceiling, cozy under the heavy arm of the sleeping Girl.

CHAPTER FOUR

✦

You Can Puke on Me

The Girl's next birthday is six weeks after the end of Bobby Dot.

Or maybe eight or nine weeks.

Or possibly four.

StingRay is not very good at measuring time. Though she wouldn't want to admit that out loud.

"It's been a bunch of weeks, anyway," she thinks to herself. "I know it's been a bunch of weeks."

As a birthday surprise, the Girl's parents buy her a new walrus—exactly the same model as before. It arrives in a cloud of pink tissue paper on the morning that is both the party and the Actual Day of Birth. The walrus is fat and walnut brown, just like Bobby Dot was, but its eyes have a flat unfocused look that make it seem more like furniture than someone to care about.

The Girl tries to love the new walrus. When she first receives it, she gives it a big hug, and in the days after, StingRay sees her cuddle it and talk to it and put necklaces on it, but never for very long. Always, after a couple of minutes, the walrus is flung to the floor in favor of something else. The Girl can't even think of a name for it—just calls it No-Name Walrus.

Even when the toys are alone, No-Name Walrus never talks. It does not even smile or tilt its head like the rocking horse in the corner. Instead, it is silent and still. Like the orca and the pirates in the bathroom.

Maybe that is why the Girl can't love it.

In fact, she seems angry at No-Name Walrus. She throws it across the room one day, sobbing, "You're not the same. You're not my walrus! Not my real Bobby Dot walrus."

One day the Girl picks up No-Name Walrus and puts him in her backpack. "StingRay wants to come, too!" she calls down the stairs to her mother. "Can I bring StingRay?"

"We can't exchange StingRay," the mom calls back. "You've had her for a long time."

"She wants to help me pick out something else. She wants to go to the store!" calls the Girl.

StingRay is not at all sure she *does* want to go to the store. She is glad she is not being exchanged, whatever that is, but the store could be full of cash registers that ding so loud your ears hurt,

and salespeople who put stickers on you,

and long ropes of licorice that people swing around their heads, and dressing rooms with too many mirrors so you see yourself a million times.

These are ideas StingRay has gathered from hearing the Girl talk about stores, and she worries about them the whole time she and No-Name Walrus are in the backpack, which is dark and smells like old fruit. But in the end, when StingRay comes squinting out into the light, the store is bright and cheerful: a room full of wooden shelves stacked with puppets and plush animals, puzzles, art supplies, and board games.

"Sure we can exchange this little guy," says the store clerk, checking the receipt the Girl's mother offers her.

StingRay looks once more into No-Name Walrus's furniture eyes and sees nothing. "Goodbye," she whispers, just in case it can understand her.

Then the clerk tosses it gently into a bin of other, identical walruses, and suddenly StingRay cannot even tell which walrus she lived with for a week, and which are strangers.

It was always a stranger walrus, she supposes. It was never going to be anything else.

The Girl is allowed to pick out a toy the same price as No-Name Walrus was. She browses the shelves of stuffed animals, holding StingRay by the tail. StingRay has never seen so many toys.

It is kind of disturbing, actually.

"Hello there," StingRay whispers to a woolly knit dolly with button eyes. "I like your blue dress."

The dolly doesn't answer.

"That's great ruffly lace," StingRay adds, friendly.

Still no answer.

It is a stranger dolly.

The Girl stops before a small plastic tiger with an angry, almost sour-looking face. "Excuse me," whispers StingRay. "May I offer a helpful tip?"

No answer.

StingRay persists, still whispering: "You might want to look a little more adorable. The goal is to make my girl want to take you home. Not to scare the socks off her with your angry toothy tiger mouth. You have to make yourself as lovable as possible. Look!"

StingRay makes her most lovable face.

No answer from the tiger.

As StingRay looks around the shop, all the toys seem asleep. Nobody moves or smiles or blinks.

The Girl touches a cuddly soft goldfish, its lips pursed in a kissy-face, its plush a sunny yellow.

(Oh! StingRay hopes the Girl won't get another fish. She wants to be the only fish.)

The Girl moves along and touches a white seagull with orange feet, plump and dapper.

(Now that she thinks of it, StingRay hopes the Girl won't get any marine animal. She wants to be the only marine animal.)

The Girl touches a floopy gray elephant.

(Truth be told, StingRay hopes the Girl won't get a

plush creature of any kind. She wants to be the only plush creature.)

The Girl should get some dominoes, thinks StingRay. Or a board game. Or a puzzle. That way StingRay will only have to share specialness and cuddles with Sheep, who really isn't that cuddly anyway.

The Girl touches a—what is it? The chocolate brown tail of Something. The Something is buried in a large pile of pink-and-white teddy bears who are staring at the ceiling, inanimate. StingRay can only see the tail of the thing, and a bit of its backside. Nothing else.

The Girl pats the tail.

And the tail waggles.

StingRay is sure she saw it waggle.

When she looks at the Girl's shining face, she thinks maybe the Girl saw it, too.

The Girl reaches her soft hand into the pile of teddies and StingRay twists her neck to get a better look. Out comes a burly, chocolaty buffalo. His nose is twitching just the tiniest bit in worry, and he looks ill, but StingRay can tell from his face that he is friendly.

The Girl holds StingRay up to meet him. "Ummmm. Lumphy. Lumphy, this is StingRay. StingRay, this is Lumphy."

The buffalo's shiny, awake eyes meet StingRay's. "Hey there!" he whispers, once the Girl has set them both on the counter and trotted across the store to ask her mother if she can take the buffalo home. "Am I Lumphy or StingRay?"

StingRay laughs.

"Because I'd like to be Lumphy," the buffalo goes on, "but if you're already Lumphy I can be StingRay, no problem."

"You're Lumphy," says StingRay, sweetly. "I've been StingRay for a while." And suddenly she doesn't care one bit about being the only plush creature, at all.

She doesn't need to be the only one.

Who wants to be the only one?

. . . . .

The buffalo gets sick to his stomach in the backpack. "Oh, oh, oh," he moans, keeping his voice low so the Girl won't hear. "This is not a good situation. There's no air. It's so dark."

"We won't be in here too long," says StingRay. "When the car goes over the bumpity part you know you're almost home."

"Really?"

"Yes."

"And what's that old fruit smell?" the buffalo moans.

"I think it's pear." StingRay sniffs. "Or maybe apple? No. Definitely pear."

"How do you know so much?"

StingRay glows. "I've been around a long time," she says. "Plus I arrived on the planet just knowing things. It was kind of like magic, how knowledgeable I was from the start. I don't think it happens to everyone."

Lumphy moans. "My tummy hurts," he says. "Do you know why my tummy hurts?"

"It's probably worry," says StingRay. "But also it could be motion sickness."

Lumphy is sick to his stomach on the way up the stairs. He is sick when the Girl bounces with him on the high bed. And when the Girl is called downstairs for dinner, he is sick just sitting still on the carpet.

"I don't think it's motion sickness," he says. "Because there's no motion, anymore."

"Are you going to puke?" asks StingRay.

"Maybe."

StingRay feels a surge of generosity. Lumphy needs help. "You can puke on me if you need to," she blurts.

"Okay," says Lumphy. "Thanks."

They wait.

Finally, Lumphy makes an embarrassed noise. "What's puke again?" he asks.

"Throw up."

"But. Ah. I thought you said I could puke *on you*."

"You *can* puke on me," says StingRay, full of simple joy at her gut instinct that Lumphy is a deeply excellent person. "Because you are my friend now. It's an honor to have a friend puke on you."

"It is?"

"It's like a huge compliment." She made this up herself, but it was so long ago that StingRay believes it now.

"Hm." Lumphy rubs his face with one front paw. "Maybe I don't understand compliments yet."

"Well. There are other ways to give them," says StingRay. "Like, you could tell me I'm an especially pretty color."

"Oh," says Lumphy.

"Or you could say that I'm your friend, too."

"Oh."

"Are you still going to puke?" asks StingRay.

"Maybe. I don't feel good."

"Go ahead!" StingRay cries. "I don't mind a bit!" Although now she is remembering that if she gets puked on she will have to go down in the basement and be washed and possibly *dried*, which actually sounds like a horrible idea. There is a terrifying pause.

Lumphy looks fantastically ill.

StingRay wonders if she can take back her offer.

No. She can't take it back.

Frrrrrr, Frrrrrr. She makes that fear noise without meaning to, again.

If she takes it back, Lumphy won't be friends with her.

He looks even more ill.

StingRay squeezes her eyes shut and waits for it.

"I—I don't think I *can* actually puke," Lumphy finally says. He sounds a bit disappointed. "Because I don't eat anything."

Phew.

"How could I forget?" StingRay says. "Of course you

have to eat to actually puke. I don't know how I could for-get that for a second like I did, because I totally know all about that."

"Sorry I can't puke on you," says Lumphy.

"That's okay."

They are silent for a moment.

"Hey. Do you know what?" asks Lumphy.

"What?"

"You are an especially pretty color," says Lumphy.

CHAPTER FIVE

❀

In Which Lumphy Is Brave
with a Tuna Casserole

During his first four months in the house, as winter rages and then melts, as spring greens and flowers, Lumphy watches a lot of television and lets StingRay teach him board games. He also spends time in the bathroom. The Girl sets him on the toilet seat cover while she takes a bath. It is there that the buffalo witnesses tooth brushing, hair combing, scrubbing with a long-armed scrubby brush, nail clipping, something called hair conditioner, braiding, and also squirting with a spray bottle.

It is all pretty difficult to understand. Lumphy's buffalo body doesn't need any conditioning or combing or clipping. He just goes natural. And all this bathroom activity seems to take an awful lot of the Girl's time every day. Some of it is obviously cleaning, but some of it doesn't make any sense. Like, why would you clip your nails? Wouldn't you want to sharpen them instead?

At night, when StingRay is asleep on the high bed, Lumphy sometimes trots down the hall to talk to TukTuk about the activities of the bathroom. Right now, he is curious about nose blowing. Where does the snot come from? It comes out in a big honk, like magic.

"I want some snot!" Lumphy tells TukTuk. "I want to blow my nose and have buffalo snot."

"I want to be ironed," says TukTuk. "But it's not happening."

"That's so unfair," Lumphy grumps.

TukTuk sighs, but doesn't answer.

Now Lumphy wants to know about the purple spray bottle. "What's the point of it?" he asks.

"People like gadgets," says TukTuk sagely.

"All it does is get the tile wet. Why does she want the tile wet?"

"She doesn't want the tile wet. She likes to work the spray bottle."

"Why?"

"Just to work it."

Lumphy doesn't think it sounds anywhere near as fun as blowing your nose.

. . . . .

The next day Lumphy, StingRay, and Sheep are helping the Girl play farm. She is doing farm chores, walking around and giving each toy a bagel chip.

The mom comes upstairs carrying a new animal against her chest.

It is an orange animal. A little smaller than the

one-eared sheep. It is stripy on the back and white on the underbelly. Fairly fluffy. And hairy.

It doesn't seem to be made of plush, actually.

In fact, it is wiggling.

In front of the Girl.

In front of the mommy.

StingRay and Lumphy have never seen anything like it.

The Girl drops Lumphy. "Pumpkinfacehead!" she cries.

"She's here for a week," says the mother, setting the animal down. "While Jessica's on vacation. I just have to get the litter box and the cat toys out of the car."

As soon as the mom sets her down, Pumpkinfacehead bolts under the bed and presses herself against the wall. "Hey there, kitty," the Girl calls, lying on her tummy and reaching her hand under to stroke the thin orange tail.

Pumpkinfacehead mews, pitiably, but does not move. "Mngew."

"Kitty kitty kitty," the Girl coos.

"Mngew."

"I won't hurt you."

"Mngew."

The Girl tries a little while longer, but Pumpkinface-head isn't coming out, so eventually the Girl gives up and goes downstairs.

"What is your problem?" StingRay scolds, as soon as they are alone.

"Mngew."

"You don't go running around in front of the people. Just stay still and quiet when they're here!"

"Mngew."

"I think she's scared," Lumphy says. "That's why she ran. Don't be scared, little kitty. We won't hurt you."

"Mngew. Mngew. Mngew."

"Doesn't it say anything else?" whispers StingRay. "It doesn't seem very intelligent, frankly."

"Do you say anything else?" Lumphy asks Pumpkin-facehead. "It's okay if you don't. We'll still like you. It's just that we're curious. And we really enjoy having conversations," he adds.

While he is talking, Pumpkinfacehead's eyes have been focusing on a bagel chip, left over from the farm game. The chip is lying on the carpet, dirty and fuzzy.

In a movement so quick it makes Lumphy grunt in shock, the kitty shoots out from under the bed and pounces on the bagel chip, then bats it across the floor, bounces it off the toy box, claws it viciously—and eats it.

"Did you see that?" Lumphy whispers.

"I'm sitting next to you," says StingRay. "Of course I saw it."

"What does it mean?"

"She's very fast. What do you mean, what does it mean?"

"Pumpkinfacehead ate that bagel chip."

"So? No one else wanted it."

"No, she *really* ate it," says Lumphy. "She's an eating type of kitty."

Oh.

StingRay ponders Pumpkinfacehead, who is now running around the room at top speed, leaping halfway onto bits of furniture and falling down, all for no reason. "She's like a people kitty. She moves like people. She eats like people. But she doesn't talk like people. All she says is 'Mngew.' 'Mngew' and nothing but 'Mngew.'"

"She's a cat," pipes up Sheep. "That's the reason."

"Of course she's a cat," says StingRay. "We all know she's a cat."

"A real cat," says Sheep.

"What does *that* mean?" StingRay asks.

"She eats," explains Sheep. "She doesn't just chew."

"Real is when you eat," says Lumphy, pondering.

"Um hm," says Sheep. "They like tuna."

StingRay thinks this idea about real and eating explains some weird things she's seen on television.

But Lumphy isn't sure Sheep is right.

He feels real.

As real as Pumpkinfacehead.

Just different.

. . . . .

It is late at night when the problem begins. Sting-Ray is asleep on the high bed with the little Girl. Sheep doesn't sleep there anymore, so she and Lumphy are watching the toy mice practice acrobatics on a fancy blue pillow with fringe. Suddenly, from under the bed, a mad orange streak zips toward the mice and attacks them with claws bared. Pumpkinfacehead nabs the smallest mouse, a gray one, and tosses it high, then flips herself around and pounces on it again when it lands.

The other mice disappear beneath the bookcase, and Sheep rolls remarkably quickly to an out-of-the-way place underneath the rocking horse.

That poor gray mouse is squeaking in terror. Pumpkin-facehead bats with her paw and the tiny rodent skids out of the bedroom, along the hall, and halfway down the steps. The kitten tumbles after it, tail over ears, then charges back, undaunted, to attack again. This time, she takes the mouse in her teeth and returns to the upstairs hall, where she hits it across the wooden floor.

Lumphy is scared. He feels sick to his stomach. But he has to help that mouse. He searches the bedroom for something to throw at the kitten. Aha! A sparkly red Mary Jane shoe from the closet. He grips it in his front paws and waddles to the hall on his hind feet.

Pumpkinfacehead is crouching, ready to spring, tail twitching and eyes darting, as the poor mouse limps across the hallway in search of somewhere to hide.

"Stop, kitty!" cries Lumphy, so worried for the mouse he doesn't care if the people hear him.

Oof! Lumphy hurls the shoe with all his might.

Clack, clack, clackally! It doesn't go far (it is very heavy), but at least it makes a noise, and Pumpkinface-head springs to one side, electrified.

Then she leaps over the mouse, over the shoe, and tackles Lumphy. The buffalo is bigger, but the kitten is a maniac. She rolls Lumphy back into the bedroom, biting his shaggy buffalo fur and thumping his soft tummy with her hard little hind feet.

OoooF. Ow.

Lumphy kicks back. He bites her ear, but his grip is not tight and she springs off him, leaps to the top of the dresser, and crouches there, surveying the room. Tail twitching.

Lumphy plays dead and stays as still as he possibly can. He wants to check the hall to see if the tiny gray mouse is okay, but he is scared to take a step. Pumpkinfacehead is sure to pounce on the next thing that moves in the room. Her yellow eyes shine in the dark.

"Mouse!" Lumphy calls. "Are you okay?"

"Still here," comes the squeak.

"I think I have a plan!" says Lumphy.

"Yay!"

"When I lure it downstairs, you hide under the bookcase, okay?"

"Okay."

Without taking another moment to think or be frightened, Lumphy runs. Out the door of the bedroom, down the stairs. As fast as his short buffalo legs will carry him.

Rumpa lumpa, rumpa lumpa.

Rumpa lumpa, rumpa lumpa.

Pumpkinfacehead is hot behind. Lumphy can hear the thumpity thump of her feet on the stairs as he skids around the corner into the kitchen. The dishwasher looms, white and ugly. Lumphy knows he has to act fast.

He wedges a paw into the washer and the door bangs down. He grabs a butter knife in his mouth and gallops to the fridge. Pumpkinfacehead is there now, skittering across the slick linoleum on her paws, banging into a cabinet, leaping onto the table and crouching into pounce position again. Quickly, Lumphy wedges the knife into the seal on the looming fridge, then bangs it hard with his forepaws.

Pop! The fridge is open.

Lumphy was downstairs during dinner. He knows there is a casserole in there.

A tuna casserole.

Lumphy scrambles into the fridge and scrunches his bulk to the back, getting himself behind the large casserole dish covered in aluminum foil. Then he pushes hard with his buffalo feet against the cold plastic back of the fridge.

OooooF! The casserole clatters to the floor.

The kitten leaps at the noise. She throws herself off the table and out of the kitchen, running a circuit around the living room several times. Then she trots back to investigate the tuna smell.

Nervously, Lumphy pushes the casserole toward the cat, pulling off the foil so she can get a better whiff.

Hmmm.

Pumpkinfacehead dances slightly to one side.

Comes forward.

Backs up.

Then she sticks her orange nose deep into the dish and begins rooting around for chunks of tuna.

While she is busy, Lumphy runs silently back up the stairs.

What to do next?

What to do?

The hall is empty. The small gray mouse must have made it to safety.

But the kitty will come back. Lumphy knows she will.

What to do?

Oh what, oh what?

Aha! Maybe TukTuk will know.

She is a wise old towel and gives good advice.

As Lumphy charges into the bathroom, words spill out urgently. "This kind-of person, kind-of kitty, I don't know exactly, it's a thing, a Pumpkinfacehead, very fast, very orange, eats things! Attacks! Got the mouse! Tuna fish! Coming back! Help!" he cries, leaping onto the toilet seat so TukTuk can see him better.

"There's a kitten visiting," says TukTuk calmly from her place on the rack.

"What should I do? It'll eat the mice for sure!" Lumphy cries.

"Be brave."

"How?"

TukTuk gestures slightly with one corner. "With the spray bottle."

"What?"

"The purple plastic spray bottle."

"Really?"

"Trust me," says TukTuk. "You are brave and you can do it."

She sounds so certain that Lumphy takes a deep

breath and trusts her. He gets the purple plastic spray bottle from the edge of the tub and lugs it in his forepaws to the bedroom doorway.

"You are a toughy little buffalo!" calls TukTuk.

Lumphy wonders if she is right.

He peers into the Girl's room. "Mice? Are you safe?"

"Safe!"

"Horse?"

A nicker comes from the rocking horse.

"Sheep?"

No answer.

"Sheep? Sheep!"

"She's safe!" comes a mouse voice. "She's just not awake."

"What about me?" Lumphy turns to see StingRay peering over the foot of the high bed. "Aren't you worried about me?"

"I thought you were asleep."

"No one can sleep with this racket," says StingRay. "What are you doing?"

"I was brave with a tuna casserole." Lumphy says it more to himself than to StingRay, and as he says it, he puffs with pride. He had not realized he had this bravery inside him. But here it is. He is a toughy little buffalo, like TukTuk said. "Now I'm going to be brave with a spray bottle," he tells StingRay.

Suddenly, no more time to talk, Pumpkinfacehead is charging—thumpity thumpity, tiny thumps of little cat feet—charging up the stairs, careening off the banister, skittering down the hall, and—

Schwerrp! Lumphy squirts the spray bottle, squeezing hard, hard with his front paws.

Pumpkinfacehead gets it straight in the face. She leaps into the air with a look of shock in her eyes.

Schwerrp! Lumphy squirts again.

Pumpkinfacehead's damp orange fur now clings to her body. She looks at Lumphy in fear and backs up, spine arched.

Schwerrp! Lumphy ignores the choked feeling in his throat—she is only a baby kitty, after all—and squirts her again. Schwerrp! Schwerrp!

Pumpkinfacehead is soaked now, looking skinny and alone in a puddle in the hallway.

"Khhhhhhhhhh." She hisses.

Lumphy waves the spray bottle at her.

"Khhhhhhhhhh." She hisses again.

She slinks halfway down the stairs and curls herself up against the baseboard. "Mngew!" she cries once, as if wishing for aid. Then falls silent and still.

Lumphy stands at the Girl's door, victorious with the spray bottle, for the rest of the night. He replaces it on the edge of the bathtub only minutes before the parents' alarm clock rings in the morning.

That day, when the people are gone to work and school, Lumphy stands there again. In the bedroom doorway, wielding the purple plastic spray bottle.

Every day, all day. And every night, all night. Lumphy is there—and he will be until the week is up and Pumpkinfacehead is taken home in the cat carrier.

Lumphy holds that spray bottle, keeping guard, even though the people scold Pumpkinfacehead for breaking into the fridge and tap her nose for punishment. He does it even though the kitten cowers in the hallway, looking sweet and meek. Even though she purrs at him and shows him her soft white tummy. He stands there. Waving the bottle and threatening to squirt.

"Aren't you tired?" asks StingRay one afternoon, from the safety of the Girl's bed.

Yes, Lumphy is tired.

"Aren't you bored?" asks the plump white mouse, before running off to play leapfrog.

Yes, Lumphy is bored.

"What are you doing again?" asks Sheep, who has forgotten the kitten exists.

"Being brave with a spray bottle," Lumphy answers.

"You're my hero," says the tiny gray mouse.

And Lumphy's chest swells.

He will stand there, even though he is tired and bored and sorry for the lonely little kitty. Lumphy the toughy little buffalo: defender and protector of the creatures in the bedroom.

CHAPTER SIX

⚜

The Arrival of Plastic, and Also the Reason We Are Here

StingRay and Lumphy are playing Hungry Hungry Hippos. The Girl left it out on the rug last night, a game in which white marbles get eaten by plastic hippopotami. Each player hits a lever to make his or her hippo stretch out its neck and chomp a marble.

StingRay is winning. Game after game.

After game.

"Why is more marbles the best?" wonders Lumphy.

"Shouldn't you stop eating when you're full? My hippo was full a long time ago."

"More marbles are best because it's winning," answers StingRay.

"Is it winning, though, if my hippo overeats and gets a tummyache?"

"Hippos don't get tummyaches," says StingRay. "Hippos think more is better because it's winning."

"My hippo is feeling sick!" says Lumphy, crossly.

Feet sound on the stairs and StingRay and Lumphy stop playing and lie cutely on the floor. The toys can hardly believe it, but nearly a year has passed since Lumphy's arrival and today is the Girl's birthday party. She is old enough now that her party is at a bowling alley (whatever that is), and when she comes in she's wearing a special dress with ruffly lace at the bottom. She putters around the room, putting barrettes in her hair and looking at herself in the mirror.

Lumphy wants to go to the party. He has never been

to a party before, and he thinks it sounds like something he would like a lot. He wonders if there will be dancing.

StingRay wants to go to the party, too. She wonders if there will be ruffly lace for her to wear.

"Honey!" the mommy calls up the stairs. "Time to go!"

The Girl grabs StingRay and Lumphy and shoves them into the backpack. It smells like—like what?

StingRay thinks it smells like sour milk. Lumphy thinks it smells like pencil shavings.

"Sour milk."

"No, pencil shavings."

"Sour milk."

"No, pencil shavings."

Lumphy nips StingRay's plush flipper with his buffalo teeth.

StingRay pokes Lumphy in the eye with the tip of her tail.

Buh-buh bump! The backpack goes down the stairs.

Whoosh! It swings out the door, and—

Plunk! Drops into the trunk of the car.

"Maybe we shouldn't play that hippo game together anymore," says Lumphy, feeling sorry and sick to his stomach. "I think it makes me cranky."

"I think it makes you cranky, too."

"Bowling will be better."

"We should definitely bowl."

Their quarrel over, StingRay wraps her tail around Lumphy's middle. They wait out the car ride together.

"Hey," says Lumphy, as the car engine turns off. "What's bowling again?"

"Bowling is . . ." StingRay pauses for a moment because she wants to give Lumphy an answer, wants to feel important and helpful, but doesn't actually know. "Bowling is when everybody drinks ginger ale from bowls instead of cups," she says, eventually. "And wears bowls on their heads, kind of like hats,

and has their hair cut in the shapes of the
bowls!

They all play drums with chopsticks on the
bowls on each other's heads.

Bowling is also when there are especially big
bowls filled with warm soapy water,
and people wash their feet in them,
which is a good thing to do at birthday
parties because then everybody has really
clean feet after,
plus new haircuts,
so they all feel fresh,
and nobody is ever thirsty because of all the
bowls of ginger ale."

"Okay," says Lumphy. "Let's definitely do that."

"Definitely."

"Although, not the washing part."

"No," says StingRay.

"Or the haircuts."

"Not the haircuts, either. Just the hats and the drumming."

"Exactly," says Lumphy.

. . . . .

At the bowling alley, the Girl opens the backpack and swings Lumphy and StingRay by their tails as the parents greet guests. When everyone is there, the children all change shoes and take turns standing in front of a long wooden pathway, rolling heavy round objects, kind of like giant marbles, toward groups of wooden bottles.

The adults yell "Strike!" and "Spare!" and "Not the gutter, not the gutter!"

A few of the children cry.

Lumphy and StingRay sit on the pile of jackets and watch. Lumphy wonders where the bowls of warm soapy water and ginger ale are, but he doesn't say anything. Instead he asks, in a whisper: "What is the point? With the round things and the bottles. What's the point?"

"Winning," says StingRay.

"How do you win?"

StingRay doesn't know, but she's embarrassed about the lack of soapy water and ginger ale and doesn't want Lumphy to lose faith in her. "Whoever's got the most round things," she answers, with false confidence.

"But isn't everyone sharing round things?"

"No."

"Oh," says Lumphy. "I thought they were, because. Um. They're sharing them. See? The Girl is using the same one the boy with the red hair used."

"They only *look* like they're sharing them," explains StingRay. "It's a very complicated thing that's going on."

"I still don't see the point," says Lumphy.

When the rolling of round things is done, everyone moves to a room in the back of the building where they eat pizza and then chocolate peanut-butter birthday cake with frosting roses. The Girl opens her presents in a flurry of colored paper and curls of ribbon.

"Will there be a new friend in there?" Lumphy asks StingRay.

"How should I know?"

"I thought you knew almost everything," the buffalo says, mildly.

"Oh." StingRay is pleased. "Well. Thank you for noticing. But I can't predict the future."

The Girl unwraps a game called Uncle Wiggily, two Barbie dolls with blank motionless faces, several glittery Barbie dresses and a shiny pink box to keep them in, markers, a beading kit, and a nightgown.

"Nobody," says Lumphy, forlornly.

"Nobody," echoes StingRay.

Lumphy thinks maybe now there will be the hats and haircuts and the drumming and washing feet, but no. Some people have seconds on cake, some people are playing with the discarded ribbon, and some people are jumping on the seats, yelling.

And then—the party is over. Each kid gets a paper

goody bag to take home. Children pull out swirly lollipops, sticker books, and red bouncy round things.

The Girl gets a goody bag, too, even though she is the hostess. When they leave the bowling alley, she shoves it into the backpack along with Lumphy and StingRay.

Once they are in the trunk of the car, the round thing in the goody bag begins to wiggle.

And roll a tiny bit.

Boing, boing!

It even bounces—tight small bounces inside the bag.

Every time it moves, it's making a papery crinkling thump.

Boing, boing, crackle!!

Crackle, boing, boing, BOING!

It appears the round thing is somebody.

Not nobody after all.

It will not stop bouncing and wiggling and trying to roll. Inside the paper bag, inside the backpack, inside the trunk of the car.

"Excuse me," says StingRay, finally. (Lumphy is sick to his stomach and doesn't feel like talking.) "Excuse me, but you are bonking us in here. There's not enough room for you to be so hyper."

"Good morning!" cries the round thing.

"It's afternoon."

"Good afternoon!"

"Don't feel bad you missed the party," says StingRay, kindly. "It doesn't really matter."

"Party party party!" says the round thing, spinning in place.

"No. You *missed* the party," says StingRay. "But don't feel bad."

"Isn't this a party?" the thing asks.

"No."

"But isn't a party when three or more people have a good time together? I don't really know, but somehow I think that's what a party is!"

"I suppose so, yes."

"Then it's a party!" cries the thing. "One person, me. Two person, the large guy with legs I can feel over on my left—"

"Buffalo."

"And three person, you, you nice soft plushy—"

"Marine animal," says StingRay.

"Mammal!" cries the thing. "And we're all here together having an excellent time. Party party party!"

"Not mammal. Fish," corrects StingRay.

"It's my first party," says the round thing, bouncing softly. "Lucky me!"

. . . . .

The Girl tries several names for the round thing.

Maria.

No.

LopLop.

No.

Snickers.

No.

Plastic! The Girl says it over and over, as if she likes the sound.

"How about Penny?" says the mother. "Short for Penelope."

"No. Plastic," says the Girl.

"Penny's a real name, but it's also cute. And pennies are round," continues the mom, as if she hasn't heard.

"Plastic!" The Girl plants a kiss on the round thing's fat red surface.

And the name sticks.

For the next several days, the Girl spends a lot of time throwing Plastic toward the ceiling and catching her again.

Blop! Blop!

Plastic actually seems to like it.

When she's not being thrown in the air or rolled across the room, and when the Girl has gone to school and the toys have the house to themselves all morning, Plastic spends her time looking through the books on the shelves. Lumphy or the toy mice get them down for her, and she reads rather quickly, even if she doesn't understand all the words.

"What is a croissant?" she asks StingRay one day.

"A kind of monster."

"Oh. Okay. And what is a snickerdoodle?"

"Another kind of monster."

"Okay." Plastic reads on.

StingRay and Lumphy are looking out the window at the guy next door raking leaves in his yard.

"Why is the sky blue?" asks Plastic after a few minutes.

"Blue is the best color," says StingRay.

"Why? Why is it the best color?" Plastic leaves her book and bounces up to rest near her friends on the windowsill.

"It just always has been."

"Why do we call it blue?"

"Because it sounds like 'blew,' as in 'I blew out the candles.'" StingRay rears up to explain better. "And everybody knows that wind is blue. And breath is blue. If you were painting them in a painting, you'd paint them blue."

"Or gray," says Lumphy.

"If you wanted it to be right, you'd paint them blue," says StingRay.

"And why are we here?" says Plastic. "That's the thing I really need to know."

"What do you mean, why are we here?" StingRay asks.

"Why are we here in the Girl's room? In this town, on this planet?" explains Plastic.

StingRay doesn't know what to say.

Plastic bounces, expectantly. "I thought you would know."

"We. We—" StingRay still can't reply.

The toys are waiting for an answer.

"I'll tell you later," says StingRay, finally. "Right now I have some important stuff to do."

"Why did you have to ask that, Plastic?" moans Lumphy. "It makes my head hurt thinking about it."

"Sorry!" Plastic rolls around him apologetically.

StingRay's head hurts, too. But she doesn't mention it.

. . . . .

That night, Lumphy can't sleep. His eyes feel sore and heavy, but he keeps thinking about the question Plastic asked. Why are we here? In the Girl's room? In this town? On this planet?

Lumphy doesn't know.

And he can tell that *StingRay* doesn't know. Which is pretty worrying, because StingRay knows nearly everything.

Lumphy's eyes stay open all night.

The next morning, when the people are away at work and school, Plastic starts asking questions again.

"What's a robot?"

"Something that's not alive but seems alive," answers StingRay.

Plastic thinks this answer over. "Are we robots?" she asks, finally.

"Certainly not." StingRay is pretty sure.

"And how come we're here, again?" Plastic asks. "I forgot what you said yesterday."

"Stop asking that!" Lumphy barks. "Stop asking how come! Stop asking why! You are making my head hurt again."

Plastic stops, like she did before. But she asks again the next day. And the next.

She is really trying not to ask, she honestly is—but she just wants to know. So, so badly. Evening after evening, the question pops out.

Why are we here?

Then: night after night, Lumphy cannot sleep.

Wondering.

Wondering.

Why he is here. Why any of them are here.

Why the mice are here.

The Girl.

StingRay, Sheep, Plastic, the rocking horse.

It is scary that StingRay doesn't know, and scary that there might not be an answer at all.

. . . . .

One Saturday night, StingRay wakes at two a.m. The Girl is breathing deeply in sleep and the rest of the room is dark and quiet, just like it always is—but something is different. StingRay looks around.

The one-eared sheep is asleep under the rocking horse.

Plastic is quiet on the windowsill.

But Lumphy is not on his shelf.

StingRay scans the room. Lumphy is not on the carpet. Not in the corner. Not anywhere.

Bonk! StingRay hits the floor. She has a bad feeling about this.

Boing! Plastic follows her. She never sleeps very heavily.

Together, they scoot down the hall and peek into the grown-up bedroom.

Nothing.

Silently, they inch to the top of the stairs.

The television is on, down in the living room.

Fwap! Gobble-a gobble-a.

Fwap! Gobble-a gobble-a.

Boing, boing, boing!

Fwap! Gobble-a gobble-a.

Bonk!

StingRay and Plastic go downstairs.

All the lights in the living room are on! Lumphy is sitting very close to the television with a dazed look on his face.

"No TV at night!" StingRay chides him. "You could wake the people. No TV and no lights. You know that."

"I need it," Lumphy moans. "I need the light. I need the TV."

"How come?" Plastic wants to know.

"Dread," says Lumphy. "I have dread."

"What's that?" Plastic is feeling rather bouncy, now that she's fully awake. She zooms around the living room.

"It has to do with too much dark. And not knowing why we're here. And not sleeping," says Lumphy. "I just need the light really bad."

"You have to turn it off," says StingRay with authority. "I'll get you a flashlight."

Plastic bounces herself at the light switches and then at the television. The TV goes off and the room falls into darkness.

StingRay rummages in a kitchen drawer she knows about, bringing back a large red flashlight and flipping it on.

They all three sit there, looking at the beam of the flashlight playing against the wall.

"Still dread," says Lumphy. "Dread and more dread."

"How about another flashlight?" StingRay rushes back to the drawer and brings another.

Lumphy turns it on. He stares at the pool of light it makes, darker and yellower than that made by the other flashlight.

"Still dread," he says, after a while.

"Look at my shadow!" says Plastic. She bounces across the beams of light. "Look at me go! Hey, do you know why shadows get bigger and smaller? Why do shadows get bigger and smaller?"

"Why are we here?" moans Lumphy.

"You should go upstairs to bed," says StingRay. "I think you're really tired."

"I can't sleep," says Lumphy. "I can't sleep for all the wondering."

StingRay is quite tired herself. She is used to sleeping all night with the Girl. But she will not leave her friend when he needs her. "Come with me," she tells him. "There's a light in the linen closet. The people will never notice it's on. You can lie in there with the towels and sheets and things."

She leads the way, even though she is a little nervous about the mean towel club that Bobby Dot mentioned so long ago. She has never spoken with any towel but TukTuk, but StingRay knows that the purple grown-up towels inhabit both the adult bathroom and the linen closet at the far end of the hall. She squashes down her fear and lurches up the stairs, pushing with her tail. Plastic and Lumphy follow.

When they get to the closet, StingRay slides one flipper underneath the door and pulls sharply. It pops open, and Plastic bounces herself at the light switch inside.

"Sleeping!"

"Sleeping!"

"Sleeping!"

A chorus of purple towels, stacked neatly one on top of the other, sits on a low shelf. Higher up are sheets, pillowcases, boxes of tissues, and rolls of toilet paper.

"Hello!" cries Plastic. "How's it going in here?"

"Sleeping!"

"Sleeping!"

"Sleeping!"

"Sorry to wake you," says StingRay, without introducing herself. "But my friend here has dread."

"Sleeping!"

"Sleeping!"

"Sleeping!"

"He *wants* to sleep. We all want to sleep," explains StingRay. "But he's scared of the dark. We have to come here so he can have light without waking the people."

"Must you have the light on?" asks the towel on the top of the pile. Its terry-cloth corner waggles in irritation.

"Yes, we must!" snaps StingRay. "I just told you he has to have light. The whole reason he came in here was for light!"

"I need light because I have dread," says Lumphy, turning around three times before lying down in the corner of the closet.

Plastic rolls over and tucks her round body into the curve of Lumphy's buffalo stomach. She hums, quietly: "Dum da DUM, da dada DUM dum dum, DUM dum dum, DUM dum dum."

"Do you know the words to that song?" asks Lumphy.

Plastic does not. "I don't think it has words," she says. "I think it's just a hum."

"Oh, please. Everyone knows the words to that," says the towel on top.

"True. I know them," says another towel.

"So do I."

"So do I." All the towels agree.

"What are they?" Plastic wants to know.

"Oh, the more we get together,

Together,

Together,

The more we get together

The happier we'll be."

The towels' voices merge in silky harmony, not loud enough to wake the people, but loud enough to fill the small bright linen closet with music.

"Party party party!" says Plastic.

" 'Cause your friends are my friends

And my friends are your friends,

So the more we get together,

The happier we'll be!"

The second time around, Plastic and StingRay join in. As she sings, StingRay scoots over to Lumphy and taps him gently with the tip of her tail.

"Lumphy," she whispers, as the towels stop singing and begin an argument as to whether they should next do "Goodnight, Irene" or "Michael, Row the Boat Ashore."

"Yes?" The buffalo is calm now, but his eyes are still wide open and his mouth is twisted in anxiety.

"I figured out the answer," says StingRay. "To Plastic's question."

"You did?" asks Lumphy.

"You did?" asks Plastic.

"Yes," says StingRay, proudly.

"What is it?" asks Lumphy.

"Why are we here?" asks Plastic.

"We are here," says StingRay, "for each other."

Oh.

Of course we are.

Of course we are here for each other.

"For each other! For each other!" cries Plastic, bouncing up. "You found the answer!"

Lumphy feels the agony and the tension rush out of his buffalo body.

We are here for each other. StingRay is right.

The toys have been here for each other. And they will be.

The dread is gone.

StingRay tucks herself up against Lumphy, tummy touching tail. The two of them watch Plastic roll happily in circles.

"You can turn the light off now," says Lumphy. "I think I can sleep."

So Plastic bounces the light switch, and comes to rest by Lumphy's head.

The towels sing, "Hallelujah."

And the toys are there for each other, in the bottom of the linen closet, at the end of the hallway.

In the Girl's house. In the night. In the town.

On the continent, on the planet.

In the universe.

Together.

Author's Note

❧

Thanks, first, to all the children who asked me what happened to Sheep's ear. Here is your answer.

The events in *Toys Come Home* occur before the events in *Toys Go Out* and *Toy Dance Party*, but this book was written last. I suspect the stories are best read in the order they were written, rather than chronologically, but I leave the choice to the readers.

Some references:

The story about the cat and the doll who live in the tree with the large collection of hats is *Fletcher and Zenobia* by Victoria Chess and Edward Gorey. It is a favorite of mine and long out of print. The song about glorious mud is "The Hippopotamus Song," originally by the comedy team Flanders and Swann and more recently recorded by John Lithgow. Sheep's "nom nom nom nom nom nom nom" chewing sound comes from the insanely popular YouTube video of that name by Parry Gripp (safe for all ages). Pumpkinfacehead is modeled on the cat Mungo Kotis, who terrorized and charmed our family when we sublet his apartment one summer.

The unbelievably talented Paul O. Zelinsky came up with the

phrase "wise old towel," which I steal here. Plus he draws all my characters exactly the way they appear in my imagination, only better. Many thanks to Anne Schwartz for her most excellent editing and support of my work. Also to Lee Wade, Rachael Cole, Emily Seife, Adrienne Weintraub, Chip Gibson, Lisa Nadel, Lisa McClatchy, Kathleen Dunn-Grigo—and everyone else who works on my books at Random House.

My gratitude to Libba, Ayun, Robin, Scott, and Maureen for their company as I wrote this book. Likewise to Bob, for online support and shoptalk. And thanks to Elizabeth Kaplan and Melissa Sarver for representing me so well.

Thanks to Ivy for the name Bobby Dot. It was originally the name of a beloved plush Christmas elf she covered with Band-Aids. I am sorry I gave it to such a horrid walrus. Thanks also to Ivy for listening to the first draft with such enthusiasm and intelligence.

The songs the towels sing are all folk songs my family enjoys singing together. My biggest debt goes to them.

The family. Not the towels.

About the Author

✥

Emily Jenkins is the author of many books for children, including *Toys Go Out* and its sequel, *Toy Dance Party*. *Toys Go Out* was hailed as "ideal bedtime reading" by the *Wall Street Journal* and "a classic in the making" by the *San Francisco Chronicle*. Emily's other books include *Skunkdog, Sugar Would Not Eat It,* and *The Little Bit Scary People*. *That New Animal* and *Five Creatures* each received a *Boston Globe–Horn Book* Honor.
Visit her at emilyjenkins.com.

About the Illustrator

✥

Paul O. Zelinsky's retelling of the classic fairy tale, *Rapunzel,* was awarded the 1998 Caldecott Medal. He has also received three Caldecott honors, for *Hansel and Gretel, Rumpelstiltskin,* and *Swamp Angel*. Mr. Zelinsky is the creator of two pull-tab books: the hugely popular *Wheels on the Bus* and *Knick-Knack Paddywhack!,* a *New York Times* Best Illustrated Book. His illustrations for *Toys Go Out* were called "superlative" by *Kirkus Reviews*. He lives in Brooklyn, New York.
Visit him at paulozelinsky.com.